Fables & Fairy Tales of Cape Verde

R. I. J. ROULHAC

Thank you
Enjoy the journey

Based on the Original Film Screenplay works of R. I. J. Roulhac

DISCLAIMER

Portions of this novel's story and characters are fictitious. Certain long-standing institutions, agencies and public offices are mentioned, but the characters involved are wholly imaginary. The view points of the stories are solely the Author's and are in no way endorsed or linked to any Cape Verdean Governmental Party, Artist, Musician or Person.

Fable : a narration intended to enforce a useful truth

Fairy Tale : a story in which improbable events lead to a happy ending (most of the time)

Fables & Fairy Tales of Cape Verde

One of the oldest illustrations of Cidade Velha, Santiago, Cape Verde 1598

DEDICATION

To my daughters Rio & Rome. May your journey in life take you to the cities you're named after and beyond. Love Daddy, always.

CONTENTS

ACKNOWLEDGMENTS

This body of work could not be done without the lifelong research and dedication to Cape Verdean culture by the late great Raymond Almeida.

Raymond Anthony Almeida was an American born (Second generation) Cape Verdean Nationalist and Loyalist. He was a fierce advocate for Cape Verde and for the causes that would lift the peoples of African from hunger, severe poverty, social and economic injustice. He worked tirelessly to make this small island nation and its people and culture internationally known, actually lobbying to have Cape Verde's name included on maps instead of left as anonymous mounds in the Atlantic Ocean.

For almost forty years, he dedicated his life and talent to finding ways to collectively improve the lives of many of the world's people existing in extreme hardship. In the early 1970's he was the impetus and founding member of Tchuba, a Cape Verdean American Committee whose sole purpose was to garner support to the newly independent (and impoverished) nation by way of organizing the Cape Verdean community to lobby Congress for Aid and support of the recent immigrant communities in the US.

Raymond was also a true American Patriot and Veteran (Vietnam Era). Some of his accomplishments include: Genesis and organizer of the celebration of Cape Verdean life, are and culture for 1995 Folklife Festival (experienced by more than 2 million visitors). Recipient of the Amilcar Cabral Award (Cape Verde's highest honor). Served as the first Counsel to the Ambassador Embassy of Cape Verde to establish its diplomatic presence in Washington. Other celebrated initiatives that actually became Congressional Legislation include, Africa Seeds of Hope and the South African Enterprise Development Fund, a $50 million fund to support entrepreneurship in Africa (the first). Recipient of the Rainbow Coalition Award for his work in Community Development.

-Arlinda Almeida, Raymond's Beloved Wife

.

1 PIRATA DI PRAIA

The History

1456: Alvise Cadamosto, an Italian slave trader and explorer, was hired by the Portuguese Prince, Harry the Navigator, to sail to West Africa. The expedition led to the discovery of the Cape Verde Islands.

1474 to 1479: During the War of the Spanish Succession, Spanish ships pillaged Ribeira Grande in Cape Verde, captured the white residents for ransom, and the blacks to be resold into slavery.

1495: Cape Verde became the Portuguese Crown Colony.
-       WorldAtlas

1582 to 1585: Sir Francis Drake, the English privateer, sacked and burned Ribeira Grande in Cape Verde. Frequent attacks by English, French, and Dutch pirates were occasions for slaves to run away to remote interior regions of Santiago Island, Cape Verde where communities of free Africans were formed as early as the mid-16th century. These people became known as "badius" from the Portuguese word for vagabond or runaway.

-       Raymond A. Almeida at the University of Massachusetts, Special Programs Department

The Story

        A subdued dusk was settling over Ribeira Grande, Cape Verde on April 24th, 1699. In the fading light, a young Kriolu man came storming out of his house, wearing nothing but his shoes and pants. A beautiful, young, Kriolu woman chased after him, throwing his shirt at his feet in disgust.

Joao, the young man, threw up his arms, "Easy Josepha, take it easy!"

"No," Josepha howled, "I will not take it easy! Cadera, cadera, cadera! That's all you ask for. I already told you I don't like it that way. If you want cadera so bad go see the jackass up in the field!"

"Woman," he replied. "You better watch your mouth before I shut it for you! I told you about talking to me like that."

"Ha," she smirked, "oh please."

"You know I've given you everything you need," he said. "I made you the best roof in the village for God's sake! To this day, you're the only one with a shingled roof! Everyone else has sticks and straw, at best! And I ask for very little in return."

"Oh please, this dump?" She gestured to their land and shouted, "I should have married a Portuguese sailor, at least he could get me a bigger and better house."

"Lower your voice," he tightly whispered. "The whole town can hear you with that loud mouth of yours."

"No," she decreed, "I will not lower my voice! You know this is how I talk and I talk one way: loud!"

Josepha turned and headed back inside the house, talking to herself, and slamming the door shut. Joao managed to wipe off some of the dust from his shirt, fasten it, and straighten up as best as he could. Shaking his head, he began to walk up the street towards town, but not before he was teased by a pair of young girls mimicking Josepha by shaking their fingers at him and giggling.

Sunlight withdrew from the horizon, slowly letting the shadows flood the village as if they were a rising tide. As Joao neared the town, life swelled in the fading light and he measured each of his steps with an exasperated jaunt. He kept his head up and puffed at the nightfall.

As Joao entered the town, he was greeted by a local, "Oye! Mr. Barbosa! I was just on my way to the saloon."

Joao welcomed him over, "Zair Silva! Shouldn't you be tending to those twelve children of yours?"

"No, no Mr. Barbosa, that's for the wife to do." Zair glanced at Joao's shirt, clearly noticing the remaining dirt. "Now, is everything okay with you, sir?"

"Huh?" Joao shook his head. "Oh, I'm fine Silva, don't you worry about the boss. You just worry about buying the boss a drink and maybe I'll think about writing an endorsement for you to the Morgados (Portuguese landowners)."

"Oh, Mr. Barbosa that would be very generous of you. I'll make it two drinks!" Joao patted Zair on the back and the two continued walking through the town. As they approached, they passed a burnt down shack, which was recently destroyed by invading pirates.

"Look at this mess," Joao sighed. "It's a shame nobody has rebuilt this place."

"Damn pirates. If it's not the English, it's the Dutch. If it's not the Dutch, it's the Spanish."

"That's the way of the world Silva," said Joao. "Learn it."

"Yes sir."

As the last shreds of light were swept away, the two men entered town. Soon, the place was illuminated by bright torches and candles from the windows. Nightlife fueled the town square in various forms.

Joao and Zair soon made their way over to their regular watering hole. All of the patrons greeted and saluted Joao as he made his way inside the establishment. He politely acknowledged them as he approached the bar and addressed the barmaid.

"Lucinda!" He waved to the barmaid. "How are you, beautiful? Good?"

"Hey stranger! I'm good, can't complain," Lucinda's eyes caught the dirt on Joao's ruffled shirt. "Looks like you've already had a rough night?"

"Aye ya Mai, I know, I know," he shrugged. "I should have married a girl from Fogo instead of Praia. I would have no problem in bed then, huh?"

"Ha! You're bad," she laughed. "I don't think your wife would like you flirting with me, especially since I'm from Fogo. So, what are you thinking? You're usual?"

"Aye!" Joao yelled. Lucinda nodded at him, turned toward a barrel, and filled a wooden mug with his favorite drink.

"Here you go, one Grogu." said Lucinda.

"Thanks, my love, tell your father I said hello next time you see him." replied Joao.

"Of course, he's always happy to see you and hear about your tales on the sea." Lucinda smiled.

"Hey, Faustino is a good man," Joao recalled. "Taught me everything I know about sailing. I wish he could still come out with me, but age catches up with us all."

Joao's mind faded back to his younger days. He was around the age of 11 making his way down a steep, sandy dune along the coast. As fast as his little legs could carry him, he traveled toward an middle-aged man that sat along the rocks overlooking the sea.

"Faustino! Faustino," Joao hollered. "I am here!"

"You're late boy," Faustino replied. "Grab that rope there and tie me a sailor's knot."

"I know, I know. Had to sneak away from my mother. Let's, see if I remember..." Joao started at the knot and began looping the rope.

"You better remember," said Faustino as Joao continued tying the knot. "How you going to be a captain if you can't tie a simple sailor's knot?"

"There," Joao finished. "That should be nice and tight."

"Hmm…" Faustino inspected the knot, "…not bad. Good job, now grab the Grogu and pour me a cup. Just a taste for you. I don't want your mother to kill me." Joao reached down and picked up a small jug with two coconut shell cups.

Joao filled Faustino's cup to the brim with Grogu and poured a shot for himself. Faustino proceeded to take the cup and down it like it was water. Mimicking his teacher, Joao tried to do the same, but the alcohol burned too hoarsely and he spat some out from his nose as he began to cough.

"Easy boy, you're not a sailor yet," Faustino chuckled. "Takes years to be able to handle your Grogu."

"Joao!" A familiar woman's voice suddenly blared from the road above. "Joao! Where are you boy?"

"Oh no, you better get going," said Faustino. "Your mother is looking for you." Joao scrambled to his feet and started to make his way back up the sandy slope.

"Thank you, uncle," said Joao.

"Meet me by the docks tomorrow. I'm going to show you around the ship."

"Really?" asked Joao. "I can't wait! See you tomorrow!" Joao returned to his mother, but not before she appeared at the edge and slapped him upside the head for running off.

"Hey old man," Joao's mother yelled down to Faustino, "I told you to stop teaching my boy about sailing. And I can smell the Grogu on him as well you, dirty old drunk!"

"The boy has to learn," Faustino laughed. "And the Grogu will put hair on his chest." Joao's mother cursed out Faustino and stormed off, pulling Joao by the ear. All in all, it was a pleasant memory. At this point, Joao couldn't even recall what punishment his mother gave him. He could only remember Faustino, the Grogu, and his sailing lessons. It was a simpler memory. Lucinda snapping her fingers at him brought his mind back to the present world.

"Also, that drink is on the house," she said. "Don't worry about it."

"No, no, no," said Joao. "I got it."

"Oh, stop it," she said. "I said it's on the house, so it's on the house. Please!"

"No, no, no prima, I got it," Joao insisted. "You don't…" Lucinda ignored his gesture and gave him a friendly wave to get lost before walking further down the bar to serve another customer.

"Who's next?" she asked the crowd. Joao let it be and gave her a smile as he took a sip of the drink. He turned around and eyed the happenings in the bar. He could see some men playing the ourinzeira game, while others gathered around several musicians playing away. As their song came to an end, the guitarist made an announcement.

"Gentlemen, gentlemen!" The man's name was Zerui. "Making her guest appearance tonight, the lovely Batukadera: Tida Preta!" He was referring to one of the waitresses walking around serving the men their drinks. She was caught off guard by the announcement and tried to ignore the chants around the bar. Of course, the men's cries for Tida to go and dance eventually made her give in.

"Okay, okay," said Tida. "I hear you. But just one song, a girl has to make her money you know."

Smiling, she put the tray on her head and began to dance her way across the room to the band. Men began to toss coins at her feet in delight. With Tida dancing the Batuku and the musicians playing lovely music, the bar was in full swing.

Suddenly, loud cannon fire and shouting erupted outside the saloon. The roof shook and pieces of the bar's straw ceiling began to fall down. Some of the men sprinted outside to see what all the commotion was about, including Joao. However, as soon as he burst through the door and out into the street, he was confronted with a wave of Spanish Privateers shooting and capturing whoever they saw fit.

Joao immediately looked for the closest thing he could find to use as a weapon and quickly picked up a large stone to throw. Unaware of his surroundings, a pirate came up from behind him and struck him with the butt of his gun. Bewildered and dazed, Joao was knocked to the ground as he quickly fell unconscious.

The piercing cry of gunshots reverberated through Joao's body and he moved his lips to curse their attackers, but no sound could leave his body. Nothing he could say was able to rise above the wailing town as it burned.
*

As Joao began to regain consciousness, he instantly realized that he was on a moving ship when his eyes landed on a single lantern swinging back and forth. A violent thunderstorm could be heard roiling above him. Soon after, he also realized that he was in the ship's hull, chained to other men. He then saw Zair from the village passed out across from him. Joao swallowed as the grim situation started to settle over his mind.

Suddenly, two pirates came down the steps, whipping and dragging a dark-skinned Kriola woman to her feet. As they grope her, the woman fiercely fought back against the despicable men. Joao was mortified at the sight.

"Get off me you bastards," the woman snarled in Kriolu. "Don't touch me! Get your hands off me!" One of the pirates whacked the woman hard on the back of her head with the butt of his gun. Her fighting stopped and she was out cold.

"The mates want a fresh one to pass around," the pirate laughed, "so this feisty puta should do the job."

"You know what they say," the other pirate made a disgusting smirked, "the darker the berry, the sweeter the juice." The pirates both laughed as they hauled the woman off to a darker part of the hull.

The only relief Joao had was that the men soon emerged from the darkness and made their way up the stairs to the deck. Doubtless, they would return eventually. As long as that woman was on the ship, she wasn't truly safe.

It was a painful affair, but Joao gathered himself and used a wooden beam to sit himself upright. He gritted his teeth as splinters bit into his forearms, but he spat at the pain. As he did, a dark African man chained next him leaned over and started to whisper.

"Est-ce que tu parles français? Parlez maintenant!" Joao didn't understand the man, but he recognized that he was speaking French. He could only shake his head in reply. The African muttered to himself in frustration, leaned back, and then whispered to Joao again. "Spreek je Nederlands dan? Ja?"

Joao still didn't understand these foreign languages and shook his head, this time even more confused. The African man became noticeably more pissed-off and threw his chained hands in the air with disgust. Not realizing that whatever move he made would affect Joao, since they were chained together, Joao's hands went up as well, knocking him in the face.

"Aye ya Mai," Joao grunted. "Aye ya Pai!" Suddenly the African man's face suddenly lit up and he leaned over to whisper again.

"Aye! Kriolu!" The man now spoke his tongue. "You're from the Cape Verde Islands, yes?"

"Yes, I'm from Praia," Joao answered. "And be more careful the next time you move. You made me hit myself in the face."

"I apologize primo, but time is of the essence." He glanced around. "My name is Moussa Torre', I'm from Angola."

"Angola?" Joao clarified. "I was just there not five months ago on a supply ship. A Portuguese Schooner: The Maria."

"Ah, so you are a sailing man then?" Moussa smirked. "Good. We need good sea men like you."

"Who's we? And where are we going?"

"We have all been taken prisoner by some Spanish Pirates. They killed many of our comrades and only chose a select few to bring back with them for the slave trade or hard labor, I suppose."

"Prisoner?" Joao was aghast. "I'm Portuguese! I'm not a runaway slave like these badius! They have no right taking me from my home. I must talk to the captain immediat–" Moussa gritted his teeth at Joao's words as he sharply threw up his hands. Their chained hands abruptly smacked him in the face again.

"Aye," Joao grunted. "I told you–"

8

"Don't ever let me hear you say something like that again my brother," Moussa's face was twisted in disgust. "You are not Portuguese! You are an African mixed with Portuguese by birth–not by choice. You Kriolus make me laugh at how you think your better than Africans because of your colonial-mix. Your straight, curly hair. Your light skin and light eyes." He scoffed at their characteristics. "Well, let me tell you something my brother, you are African. You know what the Portuguese call you behind closed doors? What they chat about when your backs are turned?" Moussa said each word with poignant disdain. "Light-skinned monkeys. You might think you're equal to them, but you will never be their equal. You are on this ship because of your features. From your African lips to your African nose! That is it and that is all!"

Joao was taken aback by Moussa's passion. Glancing around, he could see the spirit behind the African's words. Zair had the straight hair, but dark skin, and he was bound in chains. Another man had the lighter skin, but his trembling lips said everything else. He too was in chains. Joao saw his tan hands in the lantern's flickering light, obstructed by the chains.

Each of them was bound by a belief. Whether that belief was a lie for survival or the real truth of their blood, Joao was unsure. It chained them together and that was real. Somehow, whether it was a truth he'd always known, or something that Moussa unhinged right then, Joao was suddenly aware of it.

That truth gave his chains a greater weight, but it also breathed a kind of second wind into him. The newfound weight was a lock that no man could see and the second wind was an unseen link that united him with people he didn't even know.

"I am the 1st Mate to my captain: Captain Wynn." Moussa's eyes were fierce and determined. "He is one of the greatest captains to ever sail the seven seas. We were bombarded by the Spanish while off the coast of Lisboa. Even as you and I speak, we are planning to escape and take over this ship. So, I need to know if you will help us win our freedom brother. Or...will you beg them for freedom because you think you are Portuguese?"

Joao swallowed the truth like a grimy, wet spark and finally understood Moussa's painful honesty.

Therein, he agreed. "Yes...I will help you."

"Good! Captain Wynn is French and doesn't speak Kriolu, but I can vouch for you and translate." Moussa leaned back and whispered over his shoulder to a white man. He too was chained up and sitting with his back to them. After a minute of speaking in French, Moussa leaned back toward Joao. "The captain has agreed to take you on as one of his crew once we are free. He even offered you your weight in booty once we seize control of this vessel. Agreed?"

"Agreed, for certain..." Joao glanced around at their wooden prison,

"...but how do we escape from this?" Moussa slipped his loose chains under his feet and quickly pulled out a nail-sized piece of metal from his boot.

"Quickly primo," he said, "take the shard and undo my lock." Joao grabbed the shard and began to pick at the lock. He eventually got it open and Moussa was able to free himself from the rest of his chains. He quickly turned and freed his captain next.

"Don't worry primo," Moussa faced Joao again, "I didn't forget about you." He freed Joao from his chains and they both started undoing the locks of other prisoners around them. Joao then approached and freed Zair of his chains.

"Wake up my friend," Zair blinked awake as Joao shook him. "Time to go to work."

Once everyone had been freed, they each gathered what they could use as weapons. Some used the chains they were shackled with, while others used oars that they broke into sharp, splintered stakes. Soon after, they all quietly converged at the foot of the deck's door.

"Be ready my brothers," ordered Moussa, "be ready."

Joao nodded and tightly gripped the axe he found. Sweat mixed with the dried sand on his face as cold water dripped through the hatch and pricked his cheek. The aching of the ship was the only sound echoing through them as their collective group was wrapped in stony silence. Captain Wynn peered through the door's slot at a guard walking past the hatch. As the guard came back around, the captain whistled at him like he was a beautiful girl.

"Oh! You swine think I look good, do you?" The guard snarled. "Maybe your eyes need to be bashed in to fix that..." The guard undid the door's latch, but before he could swing it open, Captain Wynn and all his men burst out from the ship's hull. Each freed prisoner marched over the deck with a vicious fire in their eyes as their captors were taken by surprise.

A roaring battle echoed over the ship as numerous gunshots were met with bloodcurdling screams. It was pounding, unpredictable, and manic. After several minutes of painful cries and earsplitting gunshots, the terror and blood were gradually replaced by cheers and hollers of excitement from the victorious prisoners.

Unbelievably, their oppressors were left dead and broken. Blood and water mixed on the creaking wood, but few even noticed. Joyous victory overshadowed the storm, their losses, and the wounds.

At the helm, surrounded by those who survived the mutiny, the captain smiled with vigorous hope. Moussa stood at his side, invigorating the men with rousing shouts. Joao helped Zair rise to his feet, even as blood slowly trickled from his friend's side. The pain was clear on his face, but both men somehow knew he'd survive the storm.

The wound kept Zair from joining the cheering crowd, but Joao patted him on the shoulder as he shouted loud enough for the both of them. Their captain held up the severed head of a Spanish capturer, inciting further cheers and yells. The storm could not staunch their cries as the thunder paralleled their cheers.

"The ship is ours," cried Wynn. "Where shall we go first men?"
*

Several months later, the crew's spirits had been lifted even higher. They were well fed, nicely groomed, and had made friends along the islands leading home. Together, they had gathered supplies, plundered the unprotected ships of other pirates, and scavenged what they could from wrecked ships.

Joao had even come into his own upon the ship. After weeks of practice and honed execution, he was responsible for climbing the mast, tending the ropes, and raising the flag. Zair had trained at his side, became a crewmate as well, and tended the ropes on the deck.

"Primo," Moussa called to Joao. "The captain and I have good news for you."

Joao laughed, "A bigger share of the booty from the next Spanish Schooner we ransack?" The Captain spoke to Moussa in French for a moment. After nodding a few times in short responses, Moussa turned and relayed what the Captain had said to him.

"The captain says we are close to your islands of Cape Verde," reported Moussa. "We're approaching the island of Santiago and Ribeira Grande. In turn, you may choose to return home, if you like. We are not the oppressors who captured you. The choice is yours, brother."

Suddenly, one of the crewmates sprinted across the deck in a panic.

"Captain! White sales approaching!"

Each of them rushed over to the bow of the ship. The captain whipped out his looking glass and honed in on the approaching vessel. Moussa used his hands to block the glaring sunlight and squinted toward the ship.

"Those sails are too big to be a merchant ship captain."

"No..." the captain lowered his scope.

"It cannot be," Moussa shook his head.

"It is," Captain Wynn spat at their luck. "The HMS Poole. With good 'ol Captain Cranby at the helm. Come to collect his bounty I reckon."

We must move," said Moussa as he backed away from the bow. "All hands on deck! Hoist the sales! Joao, come here!" He handed Joao a rolled-up flag. "The captain didn't have time to say it, but he also wanted you to have the honors of raising our new flag. Hurry now, time is of the essence."

Joao sprang to it, rapidly climbed the mast, and raised the flag of Captain Emanuel Wynn. It resembled a skull with crossbones beneath its smirking jaw, and an hourglass beneath the bones. From just beneath the crow's nest,

Joao was able to catch a good look at the approaching warship. It was a hulking vessel of frightening proportions. He quickly swung back down and approached Moussa.

"Primo, these are my waters. I know them like the back of my hand." Joao pointed at the approaching vessel. "That big ship will outrun us on open water, but we can lose it by hiding among my islands. There are hidden coves where their ship will not be able to follow or find us. And, if need be, we can use the help of some Portuguese ships I used to sail with."

"Okay…" Moussa thought it over and nodded, "…I'll inform the captain. Good thinking brother!" He ran to the captain and told him of Joao's plan. The captain quickly agreed and gave the order to set sail for the Cape Verde islands. Joao took post at the helm, beside the captain and Moussa to guide them towards the islands as the English warship kept closing in on them.

"Primo," Moussa chuckled, "even if we survive this and acquire aid from the Portuguese, remember what I told you when we were cast in chains."

"I won't forget my brother," Joao smiled, "I won't forget."

THE END

Epilogue

July 18th, 1700: The UK warship, HMS Poole, commanded by Captain John Cranby engaged Emanuel Wynn's ship off the Cape Verde Islands. Cranby chased Wynn into a cove at Brava Island, but was assisted by Portuguese ships and managed to escape Poole. It is also recorded that this was the first reported piratical use of the skull and crossbones flag that would live on in infamy as the symbol for all pirates.
-        British Admiralty Records, Public Records UK

1700: The Governor of Cape Verde complained to the Bishop that marriages had been celebrated between Cape Verdean women and foreign pirates on Sao Nicolau and Santo Antao, despite the fact that, "His Majesty does not want foreigners, much less pirates," in the colony (Barcelos 1900 I:163).

1701: A royal letter directed that slave owners should cease to obstruct marriages between black freemen and slave women, which they had been doing by setting exorbitant prices for women's freedom (Carreira 1972:282).

1712: Under the command of Captain Jacques Cassard, The French destroyed Ribeira Grande, by the orders of King Louis XIV.

1770: The Capital was relocated from Ribeira Grande, and Praia became the capital of Cape Verde. Ribeira Grande later became known as Cidade Velha.

- Raymond A. Almeida/University of Massachusetts, Special Programs Department

2 SIRENA

The Story

In the not so distant future, an elderly Cape Verdean-American grandfather accompanied his young granddaughter to the Fairmount Park Horticultural Center in Philadelphia. The two were greeted at the door by the Horticultural Society's President: Ms. Brown.

"Welcome Mr. Rose and young Miss Rose," smiled Ms. Brown. "It's such a pleasure to have you here, sir. Many have come far and wide to meet the artist of our gardens' donated statues throughout the years." She gave a small bow. "Thank you for coming."

"The pleasure is all mine Ms. Brown," nodded Mr. Rose. "I'm just happy my granddaughter could accompany me for the visit. Rio, did you say hello to Ms. Brown?" He gestured for his granddaughter. "Introduce yourself now."

"Hello," said Rio shyly, "my name is Rio it's nice to meet you." Ms. Brown knelt down to shake Rio's hand and whisper to her.

"It's a pleasure to meet you, Rio," the woman smiled again, "what I beautiful name you have. I'm sure you know Rio means river in Spanish. And, well, we don't have any rivers inside, but with do have fountains. Your grandfather's statues bring the fountains to life and make them magical!"

"Really?" Rio's face lit up. "Whoa, I can't wait to see them!" Ms. Brown stood back up and ushered them inside where others were gathered. Many people began to shake Mr. Rose's hand with admiration.

"Right this way," gestured the President, "we have many board members and local artists awaiting your arrival."

After the greetings, Mr. Rose and his granddaughter were left alone to wander the gardens on their own. They approached the main Garden and right in the middle was a large, round fountain with a girl standing on a turtle at the fountain's rear. Each smoothed edge and beautiful characteristic was emphasized by the bronze stonework.

"Wow," Rio marveled. "Did you do that statue Pop-Pop?"

"I sure did honey," said Mr. Rose.

"I love her! Look at the seaweed on her and the big turtle," she laughed. "But, why is she naked?"

"Very good observation Rio," he smiled. "I call her "Seaweed Girl". And she has no clothes because mermaids don't wear clothes."

"Oh, she's a mermaid…" she tilted her head, "…a mergirl. What made you want to create a mermaid—or mergirl?"

"Ha, well that's a funny story." Mr. Rose motioned his granddaughter over to the edge of the fountain. "Here, let's sit down a bit and I'll tell you a little story from my childhood." The two sat down and adjusted themselves to find somewhat comfortable spots on the stone rim. "It all began years ago when I was about your age. We are Cape Verdean-American, but of course our ancestors weren't always American. We immigrated to America from the Cape Verde Islands. That's where pop-pop was born and grew up."

"Yes, on the island of Fogo," she said. "No, Brava! Wait, no…I forgot."

"Praia actually," he chuckled. "That's okay sweetie. So, as I was saying, it was years ago and I was a little kid…" Mr. Rose could feel the nostalgia taking him back. Memories were revealed like sunlight from beyond a drawn curtain and he reentered those days as he recalled them.

Back then, in 1985, Cape Verde was business as usual on the exotic islands. Tourists played in paradise, while the locals struggled to make ends meet. The Chinese and Europeans were investing large amounts of money into building hotels and casinos on the islands, creating and destroying the land that stood untouched for centuries. This was a tale of not only love and compassion, but of caution.

A warning not to destroy the land for greed and pleasure.

As the moon lit up the beach a young couple frolicked in the sand, drunk on love and liquor. The woman broke away from their romantic embrace and playfully rand down the beach while removing her bikini top. The man took off after her, drunkenly struggling to keep himself in a straight line. The two ran past jutted rocks and stumbled upon a sea cave, which led deep into a rocky cliff.

The woman teased and enticed the man by throwing her bikini top in his face. The two scrambled into the cave, which was hidden from plain view of the street. They began to make love under the moonlight that trailed in. As the woman straddled the man and gazed off at the sea, she was startled by the sight of a dark-skinned woman with curly black hair. The woman was gazing at her, while submerged in the water and clinging to a massive slab of rock.

"Oh my God," the woman's hand flew to her mouth. "There's a woman out there in the water!"

"Yeah baby," he said, "yeah."

"No, I'm serious, look." The straddling woman turned the man's head around to see the woman in the water, but as they both stared at the submerged figure, she quickly pushed off from the rock and dove underwater. The last thing they saw was a huge, exposed fish tale. "Oh my God, did you see that? I think it was a mermaid!"

"Boy they weren't kidding," hiccupped the man, "that grogu liquor stuff really is strong." As the hours waned, the moonlight churned over them and eventually gave way to the rising dawn. The cool, pale light was exchanged for warm, golden rays.

The village soon came to life as it always did. In that liveliness, a young, Kriolu boy emerged from his home: a small shack. Wearing dusty, torn clothes, he walked out the door as his mother yelled orders to him.

"Listen boy, don't forget anything–you hear me?" His mother asked. "We need the corn and milk. Go to town and come straight home. No playing around."

"Okay mom," said the boy, "I understand. Corn and milk. I'll be right back." The boy started to walk down the dirt road.

"Boy, did you forget something?" asked his mother. "How are you going to buy anything without money? I swear you need a good whack upside your head to wake you up." She jammed the money into his hand. "Here, take the money and be off with you." The boy gripped the money and nodded as he scurried down the road toward town.

As the cranes and trucks hoisted dirt and rubble around, town folk were making their way to work or setting up on the street with their goods of fruit and merchandise. The boy walked into town and proceeded to buy the corn and milk from several different stores. With the corn bag balanced on his head and the milk in his hand, he started the long walk back home.

As he left the town, he saw construction being done in the distance and decided to investigate what was going on. As he approached the construction site he saw a new hotel being built. In that moment, he also noticed the roads and homes that used to be there now barely standing or completely torn down.

"Wow…they really changed this place quick," the boy whispered out loud. He wondered if the old path to the lake was completely gone. It was the best fishing spot on the island and he hoped it was still accessible. Letting curiosity take hold, the boy started to head up toward the old lake to investigate.

As he got closer to the lake, he noticed the construction and debris had blocked the river running from the lake to the ocean. A once flowing river was now nothing more than a small, trickling creek. Traveling up the ridge of the creek, the boy finally made it to the top and saw the vast lake as it always was.

"Well, all looks the same here," he whispered to himself again. His favorite diving rock was still there and his fishing spot looked untouched. The boy let the heavy corn bag down and set the milk beside it. Sweating, he began to take off his shirt and sandals for a quick swim to cool down. Making his way to a giant boulder, he climbed up and did a cannonball jump into the shimmering lake.

He hollered with excitement as the water erupted around him and fell over his head in small, collapsing waves. After he swam and dove for a bit, the boy made his way back to the boulder for another leap into the water. Just before he jumped, however, he heard a sudden splash on the other side of the rock. Soon after, he could hear someone softly crying in the distance.

"Hello?" called the boy. "Is somebody there?" He decided to swim around to the other side of the boulder where several smaller rocks protruded from the lake. "Hello?" He could definitely still hear the crying, but now it was coming from the rocks. Worried, he swam up to them, gradually stepped ashore, and was then astonished at the sight of a young girl. She was dark-skinned, about his age, and crying as she kept hugging the rocks while submerged in the water. Something about her was strange. As she cried, he noticed her thick curly black hair and that she was naked from the waist up. Yet, something was stranger still.

"Hello?" he asked. "Are you okay? I didn't think anybody else was out here."

"Please go away," she pleaded. "Just leave me."

"What's wrong?" He gradually crept closer. "Are you hurt?"

"No, I'm trapped. I need to get back to the sea."

"Trapped? What do you mean? The road is clear."

"For you, yes," she sniffled, "but not for me."

"I don't understand."

"Then I'll show you." She pushed down the tears for a moment and lifted her head up. With a heaving motion, she pulled herself up onto the rock, which exposed her full body. The boy's mouth dropped open at the sight. She had a fish tail where her legs should've been. "Do you see now boy? I'm trapped here."

"Oh my God," the boy was dumbfounded. "You're a Sirena! I can't believe it."

"I hate that name you all give us," she glared. "My name is Luna. You aren't supposed to see me, but I'm going to die here–with no way back–so it doesn't...it doesn't matter now." She sank back into the water. "Nothing matters."

"Hmm…" the boy contemplated what to say, "…my name is Faustino. I've never seen a Sire…I mean, someone like you before."

"Nice to meet you. You're a good swimmer," she gestured toward the rest of the lake. "I was watching you."

"Thanks," he said. "But, what happened? Why can't you get back to the sea?"

"I always come up here, from time to time, while my mother and father hunt in the seas," said Luna. "I'm not supposed to, but it's easy to come up the river from the sea and swim back out at night without being seen." She choked up for a second before pushing it back down. "But this time, when I came up the men started doing their work. All this rock and ground started moving from their machines and they blocked off the river. Now they've been at it for days and weeks." Her eyes grew dark. "As I said, it doesn't matter now."

"Oh…I see now. Can't you walk or grow legs?" asked Faustino.

"Silly boy," she scoffed. "That's just a tale the fishermen made up. I can't grant you three wishes either."

"Oh, I didn't know. Sorry. Well, what can I do to help you?"

"Nothing, I'm afraid. I'm stuck here and I'll die here." Tears shimmered in her eyes. "I never should've come."

"Nonsense, if there's a will there's a way." He puffed out his chest with a smile. "I can carry you back down to the sea and then you'll be free."

"Carry me?" she asked. "A little boy like you?"

"Hey, I might be little, but I'm strong. I walk into town all the time to fetch water, wood, and other things." He pointed to his head and arms. "Carrying them on my head, sometimes both hands full as well. Don't let my size fool you."

"I don't know Faustino. I just don't think it'll work. Plus, with all the people around…"

"We'll wait until it's dusk and then we'll make our way to the sea. You can hide your fins in this corn sack." The boy ripped open the corn sack and emptied all the corn onto the ground. He motioned for Luna to come ashore and gently placed her fins into the sack. She listened and it took a moment, but it worked. "There! And I'll use the milk jug to keep water with us. That way, if you get dry, you can pour it on yourself every now and then." The boy proceeded to dump the milk out of the jug and fill it with freshwater from the lake. "There, all set. It'll work. Trust me, Luna."

"Okay…" she nodded, "…I trust you, Faustino…I'm just scared." The boy wrapped his arms around Luna in a hug and the two laid on the beach embracing each other. Without realizing it, the day seemed to trickle on by. The tide kept lapping over their quiet bodies, tracing the hours on an invisible clock.

Finally, as the sun began to go down, Faustino and Luna began their descent from the lake to the sea. The men from the construction site had called it a day and were leaving for home. Only an occasional passerby would wander into the construction zone or the beach below, but they were few and far between.

The two would stop every now and then to drench Luna in water or give Faustino a break. They eventually passed the thinning creek that was once a flowing river and continued to make their way through the construction zone. Each of the hulking machines that tore up the earth looked eerie in the moon's rising light.

"We're running out of water..." said Luna as she swished the jug's remaining water around.

"I know, but we're almost there," said Faustino. "I can see the beach."

"Too many people there," she glanced around before pointing a spot out. "Let's go by those rocks and caves down there."

"Okay, I'll try."

Faustino drenched Luna in the last of their water and picked her up again. Quickly making his way across the street and onto the beach without being seen, he used his last bit of energy to make it to the rocks without dropping Luna. Letting out a sigh, they finally reached the sea.

With a quiet heave, Faustino laid her into the water and promptly collapsed into the sand. His muscles ached horribly, but they had made it. Luna quickly ducked into the water like a released fish and vanished into the shadowy waters. Watching her splash and frolic like a happy child in a bathtub, he knew she was safe and free. Suddenly an ear ringing screech tore from the sea and up popped another Sirena in the distance.

"That's my mother," Luna cheered. Faustino watched in wonderment as Luna turned and dove beneath the shrinking waves, making her way out to her mother. He saw the two embrace and dive under the water again, disappearing into the pearly darkness.

"Well, I guess that's that," the boy whispered to himself with a smile. He was glad she was okay and back with her family. "Time to go back to mine." Then everything struck him all at once. "Oh crap! The corn and the milk!" He slumped onto the beach. "Mom is gonna kill me." Just then, Faustino saw a great splash again in the distance and Luna swam back towards him. He rose and waded out waist deep into the sea to meet her.

"My mother thanks you for saving me and wishes you nothing but good fortune." Luna smiled brilliantly. "As do I. You are very strong and will grow up to do great things for others. Thank you, Faustino." She swam closer to him, kissed him on the lips, and placed a small bag into his hand. "My mother said to give this to you as a token of appreciation for saving my life. Now..." she smiled, "...goodbye."

Luna flipped around and vanished into the moonlit sea once again. Faustino walked back onto the beach and opened the small leather pouch she gave him. His eyes soon widened and his mouth dropped open at the sight of numerous silver and gold coins. He closed the pouch, clutched it as tightly as he could, and ran off towards home.

Sprinting down the dirt road to his house, he was soon wildly knocking on the door. Following a torrent of ferocious steps, his mother viciously opened the door and started yelling at him. She asked where he had been, where the corn was, and what happened to the milk.

Without stopping her, Faustino simply motioned for her to calm down and look into the small pouch he'd received. Still wild with anger, she shook her head and gazed into the pouch. However, her rage quickly melted away at the sight of all the shiny coins. Tears glistening in her eyes, she began to cry and yell in praise of her son for their newfound wealth.

Mr. Rose smiled as that long, beautiful day gave way to the present. Mr. Rose and his granddaughter, Rio, were now standing in front of a different statue. It depicted a naked woman riding on the backs of various, graceful dolphins.

"So, from that day on, the boy's life was changed forever," said Mr. Rose. "And he never forgot about the strange, little girl he helped that day."

"Did he ever see her again Pop-Pop?" asked Rio.

"Only once many years later when he was a grown man. He was up in Martha's Vineyard by the Gay Head Cliffs. Thousands of miles from the Cape Verde islands he saw her appear from the water, but this time she was all grown up too and she had become a beautiful woman. He would meet her every night that summer and watch her ride the waves with dolphins at twilight until the stars lit up the sky. Then they would lay on the beach and reminisce about their times in Cape Verde and how life had been since."

Rio starred at the statue in amazement as she grabbed her grandfather's hand. Looking up, she noticed that he had tears in his eyes. She smiled wistfully.

"I hope you get to see her again one day Pop-Pop."

"I do too my dear. I do too."

THE END

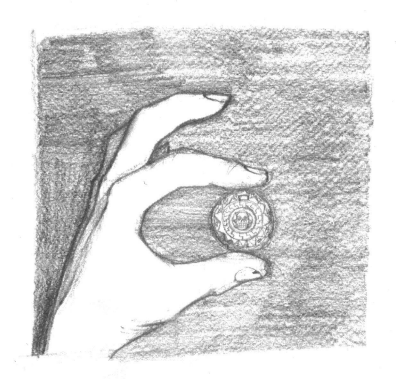

3 THE DOUBLOON

The History
"Tortuga," otherwise known as the first Pirate stronghold, has been
considered the original safe haven for Buccaneers across the seven seas.
However, only a few accounts exist which tell the tale of another Pirate
haven: the original Tortuga. It was located somewhere among the Cape
Verde islands.

The Story
The scorching African Sun heats the islands along with some of its
inhabitant's tempers. A young, Cape Verdean girl sprinted as fast as she
could from two older teens that were pushing and bullying her in the street.
"You can run as fast as you want, but we'll get your lunch money one way
or another," called the first girl.
"Yeah, go, run into the forest where you belong! You poor, dirty bastard,"
shouted another. The young girl fiercely wiped away her tears as their words
pierced her heart. Barefoot and ashy from the street dust, the girl made her
way up a familiar path. She had taken this route many times to avoid the
small-town bullies.
The lush, darkened forest began to enclose around her as the air became
cold and she ventured deeper into the woods. Twisting vines and uprooted
tree carcasses lined her path up toward the mountain's belly. Low croaks
and strange noises littered her journey through the forest, but she gradually
calmed herself.
As her path deepened, the girl began to sing to herself and make the hot,
vigorous hike pass by more smoothly. What she sang was an old tune that
women would chant while mashing corn. Familiar to her ears, it helped her
submerge the fear and worry. After an hour of hiking, climbing and
shimmying down the side of the green mountain, the girl finally came to an
opening where she could see a cove with the ocean down below.
"Well, this is a new sight," Romeia whispered to herself. "New paths lead to

new places, I guess." The young girl soon figured it would be best that she didn't wander any further than she already had. "Granted, I'll get lost if I'm not careful."

As Romeia turned around to head back down the path she created, she heard a crumbling sound under her feet, looked down, and suddenly the floor gave way. Caught off guard, she let out a scream and fell several feet below ground. Landing sharply on her tailbone, she painfully gathered herself to her feet. Once standing, she looked at the hole she fell through above her.

"Aye ya Mai," she groaned. "I think I broke my cadera. If I'm going to get out, I'm going to need to find a way up."

Looking around, Romeia realized that she was in some sort of tunnel held up by wooden beams. One way down the tunnel led out to the ocean. The other way she was unsure of. She could see small breaches in the grass covered roof of the tunnel, which gave way to patches of light that faintly illuminated it. Since she couldn't see anything she could use to climb out, she decided to follow the tunnel toward the smell of the ocean.

Feeling her way along the darkened walls, she stumbled over loose beams and rubble before noticing something shiny on the floor. She picked it up and tried to brush off the dirt as best she could, but the years of imbedded grime were hard to peel off. Still, she could tell it was a coin of some sort, so she pocketed the item and continued down the tunnel.

In time, she came to a ladder and could hear the roaring crash of the ocean waves up ahead. She was definitely curious about what rested at the other end of the tunnel, but figured it could wait till another day. As it was, she decided it would be best to leave and head home for now.

Romeia climbed up the ladder with cautious movements since many of the planks and footholds were missing or broken. Making her way up, she came to a small opening between several rocks. Stepping into it and dusting herself off, she was taken aback by the sight hanging next to her.

Tangled in vines sat a large iron cage and within it were the pale, boney remains of a person. She covered her mouth in terror, but soon realized the unfortunate soul had been dead for a long time and could cause her no harm. The grim corpse still had the remnants of some torn clothes, including a shiny, square belt buckle that was around its tattered pants.

Collecting her wits, Romeia figured that whoever the man was, he must have done something bad to land himself in a cage. Still—whether the prisoner was dead or alive—she didn't feel like sticking around. She made her way back up the ridge of the mountain and eventually found the path she made earlier. Before heading back down the ridge and into town, she covered the hole she fell through with grass.

Later that night, Romeia sat in bed with a candle on her nightstand. She was busily drawing a map on a sheet of paper with a black crayon.

Remembering where she found the secret tunnel and new path, she jotted it all down before folding the paper up and slipping it under her pillow.

Turning in, she blew out the candle, laid back on her pillow, and held up the gold coin in the darkness. She'd managed to clean it off pretty well and its reflective surface was finally peeking through. The moonlight from the window shined and bounced little reflections of light off the coin, which entertained her for the night.

*

Across the Atlantic, in the afternoon rush-hour, students hurried across campus at Drexel University in the heart of Philadelphia, Pennsylvania. Dashing through the crowds, a middle aged Cape Verdean man–carrying a briefcase in one hand and a bundle of papers in the other–made his way up a winding staircase towards classrooms and faculty offices. Winded from the climb, he gathered his breath before making his way into an office with a label above it that read: "Department of Archaeology."

"Good afternoon, Professor Cabral," said the woman in the room.

"Hello Cindy, sorry I'm late," said the professor. "Had to run across campus and grab a cheesesteak from the food truck along the way." As Cabral set his things down, he asked, "What do we have?"

"No worries," said Cindy. "We actually got a fresh delivery from Argentina! Looks like the femur bone of a T-Rex."

"Really? That's wonderful news, I can't wait to show the students and have them work on it later on."

"Also, before I forget, you have a package from Cape Verde. I left it on your desk."

"Cabo Verde, huh?" he asked. "Oh, that must be from my family." Cabral went to his desk and examined the package. "Aw, it's from my little niece–Romeia–in San Antao." He grabbed some scissors to cut the envelope. "I wonder how she's doing," he whispered to himself. Opening the package, a gold coin fell out with a note. "Hello, what do we have here?" Grabbing the coin, Cabral studied the muddy item for a moment before opening the note. Sitting down, he happily read it…

Dear Uncle John,

I hope all is well with you in America. I hope to visit you when I'm older and even go to school there like we talked about. I'm writing to you because I found this weird coin here on the island and thought you might be able to tell me what it is.

I have…

Already intrigued, Cabral looked over the coin again, but more closely this time. Upon his third viewing, he noticed something quite ancient and very strange about the coin. The way the dirt was caked over it, he could only venture a guess and opted to clean it off. He rose from his desk and approached a sterilizing sink as he equipped himself with a pair of plastic gloves.

Placing the coin in a mesh basket, he began to run steaming hot water over it for several seconds before placing the coin onto an operating table. He adjusted a bright lamp and brought it over the coin. As he did so, Cabral also grabbed magnifying bifocals that focused his eyesight. Using a sharp instrument–similar in appearance to a scalpel–he started to gently pick at and peel away crud on the coin.

As each fragment of dirt broke off and the item became cleaner, he began to move with a deepening eagerness. Whatever he was looking at, he could tell it held great significance. Finally, after several minutes of cleaning, he dropped the instrument at what he saw and his mouth would've smacked against the floor if it could.

"Oh, my Lord…it can't be," said Cabral.

"What is it? Find something?" asked Cindy. The professor took the coin and held it closer to the light. Turning it over in his palm, he examined it from every angle. He was trying to be sure–without a doubt–that he was seeing it correctly.

"Stick out your hand," he said.

"Okay…" she complied, but was hesitant, "…you're starting to scare me a bit here." Cabral carefully placed the shiny, golden coin in her palm.

"Behold, a lost piece of Aztec gold."

"What?" her eyes widened. "Whoa, wait, you mean like actual pirate treasure gold?"

"Exactly," he clapped his hands together with excitement. "What a find! My cousin is going to be so happy."

"And rich, I'd say."

"Oh, yes, and definitely rich…" he marveled at the coin again, "…I just can't believe it." Turning around, he scanned for the paper that came with it. "I should finish reading her letter, maybe there's more to it." He scrambled back over to his desk and checked the letter. It continued on…

I have been back down to the place where I found the coin and I have a feeling there might be more down there, but with my luck they are probably nothing more than old Portuguese coins. If so, they would be worth nothing now. Well, hope to talk to you soon and I'll look out for your return letter soon.

Love,
Romeia

Professor Cabral placed a hand over his mouth and started pacing back and forth. Was it possible? Had his niece actually stumbled upon such a find?

"Are you alright?" asked Cindy. "What is it?"

"I think..." he pointed at nothing in particular, "...I need you to book me the first available flight to Cape Verde, please."

"Oh," she sounded puzzled, "okay. Sure, I'll get right on that now."

"Thanks Cindy, let me know as soon as you find one." Without meaning to, Cabral held the coin up to the light again to admire it. With a smirk, he flicked it into the air and caught it mid descent. It was a marvelous feeling, but it soon changed into a form of anxiety. "I'm on my way Romeia," he whispered to himself. "If only you knew what you stumbled upon."

*

Back in San Antao, Cape Verde it was a new day. Romeia was now hacking her way through the jungle with a machete. Prepared to venture further into the tunnel this time, she also brought a circle of rope that was slung over her shoulder. As she came to the opening in the ground she had previously fallen through, she paused for a second to collect her bearings and check her things. Pulling out a map she'd drew, she took stock of the area as she mumbled to herself.

"Okay..." she scanned the paper, "...I fell through here, so if I'm right– and my map is right–the opening I climbed up from...must be..." she poked a spot on the map with her finger, "...back this way." Charting her way forward, she continued her hike through the dense jungle and folded up her map.

Before long, Romeia came upon the rocks she recognized from before along with the bones in the cage. She carefully climbed down into the dark tunnel. Once inside, she reached into her bookbag and grabbed a flashlight she'd packed. Switching it on, she brought light to the tunnel. Upon illuminating the way, she saw that the tunnel dipped toward a gradual decline.

Continuing her decent, she constantly scanned the floor for more coins, but she couldn't find anything. Up ahead she suddenly noticed two skeletons lying on the floor. Each had torn clothes and their old leather boots were still on. Shaking her head, she came close to examine the remains more meticulously.

Running her flashlight over their bodies, she noticed old belt buckles, hats, and daggers still fastened to them. Furthermore, some of the skeletons' fingers still had ruby embedded rings on them. The rosy stones dangled from their knuckles like small, crimson stars. She lifted her flashlight to glimpse their faces, but was surprised when she noticed that both their heads were punctured with a hole, as if they had been shot.

Swallowing her grim surprise, Romeia wondered what the two men must've done. Suddenly, an elongated centipede skittered out of one of the holes in the skeleton head and it startled her. She jumped back reactively and clumsily tripped forward, landing on her face.

"Ugh, ow..." she stammered, "I hate bugs." Beginning to lift herself, she actually noticed a tightly stretched wire in front of her nose. It was close to the ground and remarkably taut. She wondered what it was doing here.

Still balanced on her stomach, she shrugged, reached out, and plucked the tight wire. Suddenly, a booming crack of noise rang out and the line whipped away, sending a huge tree trunk—with spikes sticking out of it—down from the tunnel ceiling. The vicious trap swung right over Romeia's head, just barely missing her. After a few moments, the swinging momentum of the log stopped and she carefully slid out from underneath it to stand up.

"Well..." she took a deep breath, "...that was close." She figured the last two guys weren't so lucky. Almost instinctively, she waved at the skeletons with a smile. "Thanks for the heads up." Grabbing her flashlight and bookbag, she continued down the shadowy tunnel.

*

Meanwhile, Professor Cabral was on his phone talking to someone. He was sitting in the waiting section with his carry-on bag at the airport. Shaking his head, he lowers his voice and brings the phone closer to his mouth.

"I know, I know, but I don't think Romeia realizes how much danger she's really in." He absentmindedly listed the issues with his fingers. "One, if any of the local banditos find out about her discovery, she is done for. Two, if anyone from the town or local government finds out about her discover, she is done for. You understand?" He sighed as the voice spoke back. "No, nobody can know about this until I get there and take up the matter with their President. Only then will she have the necessary protection to not only claim her share of the treasure, but also not be harmed." The other voice responded and Cabral nodded. "Yes? So, I'm on my way now and I'll be there in the morning or afternoon. I already sent their President an email about the circumstances and he said to bring her to his office as soon as I get ahold of her." As the other voice on the phone spoke, Cabral heard his flight's boarding call over the intercom. "Alright—listen—I have to go, my flight's boarding. I'll email you once I get there. Yeah, talk to you soon."

The professor hung up and quickly made his way over to the boarding gate.

*

Meanwhile, back in Cape Verde, Romeia continued her descent into the twisting, handmade tunnel. Some parts were wide and other parts were so tight she had to crouch through them. She began to sing to herself to pass the time and calm her nerves when unexpectedly the ground suddenly gave out beneath her. For a split second, she was freefalling, but then she jerked to a halt. The jolt shocked her and her neck ached from the whiplash.

Blinking and shining her light around, she realized she'd been trekking across a false floor that was several feet wide and long. Still suspended, she looked down below to see large, sharpened wooden spikes sticking straight up towards her. Turning her head, she saw that her bookbag got snagged on a thick, exposed root.

That was the only thing between her and an excruciating painful death. With bated breaths, she cautiously maneuvered around and climbed out of the hole. Once back up on the tunnel ground, she let out a deep sigh and leaned against the wall for a second.

"Another close one," she gradually straightened and marched onward, "God is good." Seeing no way across, Romeia scanned the tunnel to gauge her options. Then she noticed some beams above her and the pit of spikes. Nodding to herself, she took out her rope and tied one end to the ceiling beam.

Yanking on it a few times, she hoped it would hold her weight. Taking a few steps back, she rushed forward with the rope in her hands, swung across the pit, and landing on the other side with a rolling thud. She cheered internally at her success and laughed it off. Soon after, she tried to shake the knot loose, but it wouldn't come undone.

"Oh well," she shrugged, "I guess you're staying here, my friend." She gathered herself, flicked her flashlight back on, and continued down the tunnel at an even more cautious pace. After several more twists and turns, she came upon a spacious opening which led to another portion of the cave. She also noticed that the handmade tunnel had finally come to an end. The cold air from the cave sank into her bones and made her shiver. With chattering teeth, she pulled out a blanket from the bookbag and draped it over her shoulders before sitting down with her back against the cave wall. She figured it was a good time for a break.

Romeia took out some bolacha cookies and a bottled water. It didn't take long for her to eat all of them and she found herself wanting to rest for a minute. She laid her head back and closed her eyes for a bit. The exhaustion quickly overwhelmed her and she fell asleep in the pitch-black tunnel with her flashlight still on.

After a time, piercing shrieks ripped across the tunnel walls and Romeia snapped awake. She fumbled for the flashlight and her bookbag before scampering to her feet. Listening hard, she soon recognized the shrieking as bat cries and gradually relaxed.

Now rested and confident, she threw her bag over her shoulders and traveled deeper into the new cave. Eventually, crudely sculpted stone steps began to emerge on the ground. They led her downward as the sound of rolling waves crept over her as well. The crashing waves meant she must be getting closer to the seaside cove.

Carefully making her way down the cavern, Romeia ducked under cobwebs and dilapidated stonework. As she did, she began to see more skeletal remains of half-dressed men from long ago. Suddenly, she saw the floor begin to shine when her flashlight's glow hit it. Astonished, she rushed forward and picked up one of the shiny pieces on the floor.

Holding it up to the light, she was elated at the sight of another old coin similar to the one she'd uncovered before. She began to gather them in her bookbag before continuing further into the stone cavern. After several more winding steps, she noticed that the footing was becoming more difficult, slippery, and wet. Suddenly she lost her footing, fell on her butt, and began a rapidly sliding descent down the slick rocks.

With a splash, she landed face first in a shallow puddle. Wiping off the water and coughing for a second, she lifted her face to gaze upon the new place she'd stumbled into. Rising to her feet, she was astonished to see that she was now in a vast cavern with mile high ceilings all around her covered with stalactites. A large hole in the stone ceiling above was letting in moonlight. Moreover, before her laid the most beautiful site she'd ever seen.

Dozens of small huts and houses made from wood, stone and mud sat before her with ancient, gigantic sailing ships docked on platforms. The decrepit town had winding cobblestone pathways with rudimentary street lanterns along their sides. It was clear that this was once a bustling town, but now it was nothing more than a shell of its former glory.

Romeia began to walk up the town's main street and was speechless at the old artifacts and treasures that had been left unguarded. Chests filled to the brim with pearls and silks. Inlaid golden cups overflowing with rubies and emeralds. Even thousands of her shiny gold and silver coins paved the walkways and were stored in busted parchment sacks.

Several rats scampered past her movements through the town and the sounds of old, creaking wood interrupted the roar of the waves every now and again. In the middle of her exploration, she came to a building that resembled a church with a large iron bell fixed atop it. Coming closer, she brushed the dust off its hanging door sign and it read: "Haven To All."

"God, I wish I'd brought a camera," she scoffed incredulously. "Folks will never believe this." Romeia continued to investigate all the little houses for further loot and the like, until she came to the end of the town. From there, she could see hundreds of rowboats docked up along the shoreline and a massive cave opening leading out to the sea.

Knowing that she couldn't go back the way she came, especially carrying everything that she had gathered, she started investigating the rowboats at the make-shift docks. She figured that surely one of them had to be in relatively good condition after all these centuries. After checking a few of them, she flipped one over that actually managed to float well. She then searched around for two oars that weren't broken or eaten through by termites.

With her boat then ready, she was all set to fill it up with numerous bags of pirate treasure. Unfortunately, most of the old sacks busted open when she picked them up, spilling its golden and silver remains all over the ground. However, others were still in good shape, so she packed several of those on the boat.

In one of the houses, Romeia found several women's robes and clothes from different parts of the world. Excitedly, she first grabbed a middle eastern tunic and wrapped it around her waist before draping an emerald-shaded Asian robe around her shoulders that tied off at the waist. Lastly, she put on a large, triangular, leather hat with a giant peacock feather sticking out of its brim. In that moment, she wished she'd had a mirror.

Satisfied with her expedition, she pushed the rowboat into the water and jumped in as she grabbed ahold of the two oars. She began to paddle out and toward the yawning cave mouth's opening. While rowing, Romeia gazed at the hilly maze of treasure filled homes on the shoreline. The myriad of riches shimmering in the moonlight resembled golden dots against an azure portrait of shadows.

*

Finally arriving in Cape Verde, Professor Cabral left his flight in a whirl of exhaustion. Blinking away the tiredness, he kept his composure and continued forward. The sun was rising over the sea as he stepped off the plane and made his way to a taxi.

"Good morning, my friend," said Cabral as he waved down a driver and hopped in. "Please take me to the port authority, I need to catch the first vessel over to San Antao island." The cab driver nodded and took off toward their destination.

Whipping and honking the taxi through town, they soon reached the port authority. Cabral paid the man, thanked him, and ran across the dock toward the ferry ship. He saw several men working on the ferry, while a small sign was hanging beside them that read: "Temporarily Under Construction".

"Hello! Hello! Is the ferry working my friends?" asked Cabral. "I have to get to San Antoa right away."

"Sorry friend, we're down for now," replied one of the workers. "Hopefully we'll have the parts replaced tomorrow." Then it appeared as though something occurred to the man and he gestured to another area across the dock. "Actually, you can always grab a ride to the island on one of those fishing schooners," he chuckled. "That's assuming your stomach can handle it."

"Thank you, my friend," said Cabral as he turned and darted across the dock. He was soon asking several fishing captains if he could catch a ride over to the island. The first two refused, but the third agreed to it for a nice price. Without a moment's hesitation, the professor jumped into the fishing ship and was ready to go.

Soon after, off they went. They bumped up and down in the morning waves, drifted over the rolling currents, and smacked against the larger, occasional surf. A little under an hour into the rough sailing, Cabral leaned over the side and barfed out all of his airplane food. The captain laughed and patted him on the back.

"You did good primo," said the Captain. "Gotta admit, I'm surprised you lasted this long on the rough seas. It's not of everybody."

"How…" Cabral wiped his mouth. "…how much longer until we get there?"

"About 30 minutes, my friend. You see it there to our left? It's the small island we're approaching quickly." Cabral squinted his eyes, he could see the island approaching ever closer as they rode each bouncing wave. He checked his cellphone for a signal and was astonished that he had one out in the middle of the ocean. Taking the chance, he emailed the President of his whereabouts and arrival time.

A moment later, the captain handed the professor a jug. "Here, have a swig of this. It's Grogu–made it myself." Cabral took a swig of the strong alcohol and thanked the Captain. Suddenly, his cellphone beeped with an alert. He checked it and saw an email back from the President of Cape Verde. The message informed him that a team of police escorts had already arrived at the port in San Antoa and were awaiting his arrival with his niece.

"Excellent," he whispered to himself with a smirk. "Captain, I think I'll have another swig please. Just to help calm my upset stomach"

"I thought you'd say that." The Captain laughed as he handed Cabral the jug and the two began their final ascent to the island's docks. Before long, the captain was perfectly lining up the ship so it could smoothly travel into the dock. He proceeded to jump out and quickly tie off the boot to an anchor on the dock.

"Okay, my friend, we made it," shouted the Captain. "Welcome to San Antoa's Port!"

"Thank you again sir," replied Cabral. As he gathered his things, he could see the police escort walking down the dock to greet him. Suddenly the Captain let out a whistle and began pointing toward the cliffs alongside the docks.

"Aye ya mai! Pirata!" said the captain. "My, my look at that old boat. Who is that coming this way?" The police and Cabral stared puzzlingly at the anciently dressed figure approaching them in an old rowboat. Somehow something clicked and Cabral put it all together in an instant. When he did, he ran down the dock and jumped off onto the sandy beach toward the boat yelling and waving.

Perhaps–deep down–it was the pirate hat that gave her away.

"Romeia, it's your uncle," he called. "I'm here! Romeia it's me!" She recognized Cabral right away, but was shocked that he actually came all the way to Cape Verde. His niece waved back and she continued to row as fast as she could toward the beach.

John and the captain, along with some police, waded out into the water to help her. They banded together to guide her rowboat inland. Once firmly ashore, Romeia leapt into Cabral's arms and nearly knocked him over.

"Uncle, I can't believe it's you," she said. "You came!"

"Yes, yes I got your letter," he said. "You found something very…" Just then, he caught a glimpse of the pirate treasure in the boat Romeia brought with her. "…oh my God! What have you found, my girl? I can't believe it…"

Cabral gleefully dipped his hands into one of the bags of coins and let them run like water through his fingers. It felt as if a legend was resting in his palms. The police and captain were also shocked by the sight as they began to shout and wave for help from ashore.

"My dear you may have just uncovered the largest treasure site in the history of the world," said Cabral. "Did you realize that? You're gonna be rich!" The two embraced and he carried her onshore as the other men pulled the boat onto the beach.

The police began to control the area as townsfolk approached by taping it off and keeping anyone too curious at arm's length. As they did so, the authorities also carried the bags of treasure back up to the docks and into their vehicles. It was a gradual haul, but they quickly accomplished the task.

Cabral and his niece were ushered into another police vehicle as word began to spread among the congregating townsfolk. Romeia even saw the two bullies from town glaring at her from the sidelines. She reached into her bookbag, gathered a couple of the coins she once used for lunch money, and threw them to the bullies with a smile.

"Here you go," she smiled. "Enjoy your lunch, it's on me." The two bullies could only stand there looking dumbfounded as Romeia waved goodbye. As the police escort rushed off the docks and carted them through the town, she found herself smiling and thinking of the lost pirate haven she was leaving behind. In the rising sun, she could only imagine the moonlit portrait in her memory coming to life with warm sunlight.

An old, golden world reborn.

THE END

Construction in Santiago, Cape Verde 2019

CREDITS/REFERENCE

1598-1599 Map of Praia "Vera Delineatio Ca- Stelli Praia courtesy of The Cape Verdean Museum Exhibit. 1003 Waterman Ave, East Providence, RI 02914.

All sketches/artwork featured done by Graphic Artist, Alberto Hipolito Fortes

Photo of Cape Verde courtesy of Musician, Zerui Depina

Historical Facts

-Raymond A. Almeida, University of Massachusetts, Special Programs Department

-WorldAtlas.com

-British Admiralty Records, Public Records UK

-Barcelos 1900 I:163

-Carreira 1972:282

GLOSSARY

Cadera - Butt

Oye - Hey

Morgados – Portuguese land owners

Grogu – Sugar Cane Rum

Ourinzeira – Counting game played with a board with holes and seeds

Batukadera – Professional dancer of Batuku

Batuku – Cape Verdean traditional dance

Aye ya Mai – Oh my Mother

Aye ya Pai – Oh my Father

Kriolu – Official language of Cape Verde, Portuguese and African mixture.

Primo – Cousin

Banditos - Thieves

Pirata - Pirate

ABOUT THE AUTHOR

R. I. J. ROULHAC is founder of "The Cape Verdean American Film Festival" & the award winning online talk show "Coffee with Kriolas." Rashad Isaac John Roulhac was born in New Haven, Connecticut in 1977 to two Quinnipiac graduates, Edward Thomas Roulhac from South Bronx, New York and Sandra Jean Rose of Cape Cod, Massachusetts. Growing up in Yeadon, PA (the birthplace of Flag Day) Rashad has always been inspired by 80's pop culture, fantasy and history. His favorite quote is Albert Einstein's "Imagination is more important than knowledge."

Made in the USA
Columbia, SC
12 September 2019